No Man's Land

No Man's Land

MATHEW JOSEPH

PARTRIDGE

To order additional copies of this book, contact
Partridge India
000 800 10062 62
orders.india@partridgepublishing.com

www.partridgepublishing.com/india

FROM THE AUTHORS TABLE

All living things have a SOUL, and also, the dead living things do have soul, Rivers, oceans, forest, mountains, desert and all nations, planets and stars too. All soul choose and decide their own plan for the future and they make the shape of the body as well as they choose to have a life with the pain or pleasure in next life. Some give pain to others some accept pain, likewise some give happiness and pleasure to others and some do otherwise. But the beauty of it is that all keep churning and keep rotating their body and shape and churn the life and experience to move forward to get in to emancipation. The target is the mother soul who is the THOUGHTS (some may call its GOD) from all these fragmented tiny soul sprouted and started the journey. Finally all will reach back into that mother thoughts and become one single thought again.

IF I AM IN YOUR THOUGHTS, THEN I AM ALIVE.

INTRODUCTION

This book is purely the conversation overheard from two aliens who visited this planet for their routine study from an another planet. Their life and knowledge are not based on the senses, like we are used to. They see and perceive in different ways.

This book is pure fiction. It might have certain similarities with human life. Human beings have their limitations in thought processes and imaginations. All our knowledge and learning purely depends upon our senses. We do not have an idea of how space will be or what TIME is. We can only imagine it with our senses. If one wants to measure TIME or SPACE, one has to imagine the starting object and the ending object and measure the spaces between these two objects. Without these boundaries, our brain and senses cannot think or understand anything. (our brain is not matured enough to understand Time and space. But the soul might be able to understand it, but, we refuse to look at our soul and we are completely at the mercy of our brain.

Whoever wants to accept this book as his or her story is welcome to do so. It can be an acceptance of the perception of those two aliens and their teachings to their junior.

PREFACE

'No man's land' is a country with people who keep claiming their past culture and traditions as they don't have anything good to talk about the present, and nothing good to claim in the present. Therefore, they conveniently prefer to live in the past.

Yes, they have had a great past and great history but it is all 'ONCE UPON A TIME.' Their forefathers were very tolerant and they used to accept new ideas. For example, few thousand years back a person called Thomas reached here from a faraway land with new ideas, new teachings and new beliefs. Few people accepted and adopted, some others respected these ideas. The locals accepted the people, who came to this land, gave them refuge and helped them settle here. In fact, their culture was called HINDUISM. This was accepted and they lived respecting each other.

The land is full of sycophants and cowards. They proclaim they are tolerant, but in reality, they are not. For example, a pretty girl walking on the road with a minimum exposure of her body will cause the people to turn violent and results in the girl being harassed for only doing what she felt natural to do.

This entire book is about what I overheard from the discussions of two aliens who stopped over here for the study tour, and what you read here is completely their perceptions and views. You can have your own perception and beliefs—. As in this no man's land, people have hundreds of perceptions for a simple point, and continue to churn with it over and over again as they don't want to face the truth and confront it.

For example: There was a rape case, which shook this no man's land and the entire world. In a documentary that was made by the BBC on this case, a lawyer of the accused was seen arguing that if his daughter goes out at night for watching a movie, he shall burn her in his farmhouse! Well, he wanted to inform the world that he has a farmhouse, and he correctly nailed it, didn't he? Also, his perception of a gang rape was established through his speech.

The second lawyer claimed his tradition is the greatest in this world. The girls are like rose petals, whereas boys are thorns! A lady judge in the TV interview claimed that her land boasts of the greatest culture in the world, and everything is going to be just fine if people are educated. (Does she have the faintest idea about what her colleagues and lawyers just said? Or is she assuming those lawyers are uneducated?)

The thunder struck when a journalist asked the lady judge about her biggest liability and tension in life. She replied, 'it is her daughter.' The TV channels spend hundreds of hours hosting the discussion room with experts and the subject being rape. Companies gladly spend millions to sponsor the discussion on RAPE. Look at the irony of it. This is why the outer world just cannot understand this so-called great culture, which they claim to be perfect and proud of "—" but proud of what?

CHAPTER 1

Earth Beckons

Isabella is worried. Her son Thomas is going to No Man's Land on Earth, with John for an expedition. And she believes that No Man's Land is an abode of chaos and calumnies. Isabella's late husband had been there, and she feels that the land is dangerous, does not want little Thomas to go there. Naturally, Isabella is worried for his well-being and safety. No words can explain her feelings.

'She prayed 'LORD',_you are our savior, our great king, and I beg you to change your decision to send my dearest and only son for an expedition to the Earth. I have heard from my late husband that it is very far from our planet, and that the inhabitants who live there are much inferior to us. It is a primitive world that they live in. As you are

1

well aware, my late husband has worked for millions of years and has done many expeditions that are similar to this. Our entire kingdom has been benefitted from his study and research.

'Therefore, I beg you once again to relieve my son from this earthly expedition.'

John is unmoved. He understands Isabella's worries. 'But' he replied that, 'experimenting, voyaging, and navigating are the duty of our science division. You cannot escape that. We should keep traveling to all stars and their satellites to study their progress, and we need to learn and combat with them to maintain our superiority.

'My dear lady, I completely agree with you, and I appreciate the great work that your husband has done for all of us. Yes, we all are much benefitted from it, and we all must thank him for his great work forever. But I wish to inform you that I have thought in great depth about sending your son for this particular expedition, and there are various reasons for it.

Earth is not too far away from our place and it is only a few billion light years as per an Earth inhabitant's calculation. For us, it is only a few days traveling distance.

Earth inhabitants are primitive compared to us, and they are still in the era of materialism where they are completely dependent on their senses.

They can neither see nor feel us. Therefore, we are not in danger nor are our security threatened by them.

I am sending one of our senior scientists along with your son. He has traveled with your husband to Earth. He has good experience in these kinds of expeditions. Therefore, your son can learn much more under his guidance.

'Let him go and explore. The universe is ours, as we are in control of many stars and its satellites along with the inhabitants.'

CHAPTER 2

In Search of the Unknown

John and Thomas stepped foot on Earth. This is Thomas's first travel, and his eyes are wide open with excitement. He is going to see, feel, and experience new things. But he does not seem to be pleased with the first look. Thomas is all set to witness new things that are different from where he comes from. Thomas is filled with curiosity. He has a million questions to John. Thomas shoots. John has all the answers.

'Where are we sir? This place stinks. Who are those souls scavenging in that pile of dirt and waste?'

'Yes, we are in our targeted planet Earth. To be specific, we are in a city which is part of a country called no man's

land. Let us get started with our study tour. I also want
to inform you that we will see all sorts of souls out there,
but none of them can see us nor feel us,. These people still
live in the primitive era, and they have to depend on the
senses to know, feel, and hear others.

"Okay, I get that! But what are these souls doing in this
heap of rubbish?," asked curious Thomas.

"These inhabitants have categorized themselves into
higher and lower levels. The lower levels have their
boundaries, (as there are higher and lower standards
of souls). The human beings here carry the different
standards of souls. Therefore, their behavior and
understanding are totally different. Also they have
divided people according to their standards of life, which
are based on these boundaries. In earlier times, they used
to divide people according to different castes and religions.
But recently, they have been doing it with a new method
or a medium called "money". Also the earth is divided
into many nations according to the color of the people.
The highest standard souls mostly take birth in the white
colored world, the second lot in yellow colored, the third
as black colored. The balance constituting tan and brown
colored have mostly taken birth in this no man's land to
see the worst and do the worst. Again, among the last lot
too, there are different standard of souls., and they create
many divisions and standard among themselves. Now, let
us move on to their cities," suggested John.

Chapter 3

Driving in No man's land

Why these roads and canals are extremely filthy when compared to the other side of Earth, where white colored souls live; and this whole place looks like a war zone. Why are vehicles moving too fast in narrow roads, and where are they all hurrying to? Why can't they go in a straight line? We saw it like that in the other parts of the Earth.

'My dear, those vehicles are a creation of those white men—specifically the western people. It was developed according to the western brains and standards. They are evolved and are at much higher levels. But people in this part of the world have not yet reached those standards. But the westerners are selling their products here for their benefits, and it is something called money! The person who is driving a vehicle here has not yet reached the level of the vehicle that is moving at a faster speed than his brain! Their mind still works and matches only in bullock cart speed.

'A bullock cart is pulled by an ox. On the other hand, a person here sits behind the steering wheel of a car, while their primitive mind does not match and fit into that technology or speed. They get excited, and the next thing they do is to accelerate to the maximum speed that the car can pull off! Look at how these vehicles race! One wants to go in front of the other. Do not misunderstand that the person in the vehicle behind is in a hurry, or that he has to reach his destination in an emergency. In fact, if you take a closer look, you can understand that the one who is behind the car and the one who is honking to go ahead of the other car is as clueless as you and me about why he wants to go so fast. He does not have to reach immediately nor does his boss who is sitting behind him! His ignorance coupled with his underdeveloped standard does not match the speed of the vehicle that he is controlling.'

Youngsters speed in their fancy cars and bikes that are made and developed in western countries. Why do they forget themselves once they get in those seats?

There is no difference in the behaviour of the rich or poor. All are equally bad or compete with each other in this respect. For example, some crooked people make money by selling the western products to others and then they don't know what to do with the new richness. Mostly, they buy the most expensive cars from the West and give them to their young boys. Basically, the parents don't understand these cars are made for the developed mind and only those who can manage them can enjoy their comfort. But the boy who got it gifted from his parents drives the same vehicle as if there is no tomorrow. In fact, those vehicles are made for wider and long roads, so that they can run at high speeds. But here, there is no road in reality. Whatever is there is full of pot holes and pedestrians and street sellers. This ignorant rich man's son cannot understand, and he forgets himself when he sits on this vehicle and he drives around madly and often kills and knocks down the pedestrians.

'Take a look at those people who are standing next to the three and four wheelers. They are called taxis, and they are waiting for customers whom they can drive for a short distance. And they get paid for it. That too, only for a fixed amount. They chew tobacco, spit all over, and laze around, but when a customer sits in his vehicle, he can see these taxi drivers speeding through the roads. You would wonder why they are over speeding. The customers do not question either. But he does not want anyone else on the road or ahead of him, not even a pedestrian. He stares at the pedestrian with an angry look as if he questions his right to walk. He will keep honking and hooting as if he is in an emergency, at last he reaches the destination of the customer and he gets paid. But he has taken so many risks of colluding with other vehicles, and he was about to hit a few pedestrians too for this small fixed amount (he has no idea nor any brain to understand and evaluate what he was doing in those few minutes of journey). He can again be seen standing with the vehicle as a normal man. This shows that the vehicle did not suit him, however if you give him the bullock cart to drive, it would have suited him and he would have had a smooth ride. These things you can notice in everyone who lives in this no man's land including the rich and self-proclaimed educated. But in reality, all are same.

Basically, in terms of evolution, people in 'no man's land' are thousands of years behind their counterpart— the westerners. They cannot match with the speed or technology of the western world with their bullock cart state of mind!

While walking on the road, everyone behaves extremely normal. But when the same guy gets to sit on a driver's seat, he does not want any pedestrians on the road nor can he stand any other vehicles in front of him. He conveniently forgets that he was a pedestrian a few minutes back! Also, that he has to be one amongst them after a few minutes. Even if an old person is seen crossing in front of him, he keeps hooting and blowing the horn, so that the entire road and space is available according to his convenience.

When the traffic is moving and if a car has to slow down due to some obstacle ahead of him (maybe a hump or an old lady trying to cross the road), the vehicle behind the car immediately moves toward the right or left just to avoid the slowing car. He just wants a small gap to flee! He feels that the others in front of him who reduced the speed are either stupid or blind.

In other parts of the world, people look for quietness and silence, but in this land they encourage noise. Most of the vehicles carry a message HORN OK PLEASE. You can only get to see it in this land, (they are asking and requesting others to hoot and honk.)

Why do authorities give permission to drive like that?

'It is not a herculean task to get a license in this place. Don't compare the difficulties and training required on the other side of this land with how it works here. You can easily avail a license by giving a few hundreds of their currency. They need not pass a test nor do they need to be educated about driving etiquette. Hence, they prefer shutting their eyes. The extra income that will land in their pockets are more important than road safety.'

Now, the authorities are making new rules for penalizing individuals for breaking the rules, but they refuse to teach the drivers how to drive and how to safeguard the pedestrians, etc. Basically, they want the drivers to be ignorant of rules, and they expect them to break the rules so that the authorities can make money out of it and act like God for them. It is easier to take a driving license and kill a person in this land than taking a license for the gun to kill a person.

But look at the roads. There are parked cars on either sides, and there is hardly any space for a person to drive his or her car.

'Here, authorities allow development of buildings without a proper master plan. What you have seen in the western world are planned cities. They plan and develop everything as per the specific needs and requirements. They plan for the proper wider foot path and better roads and better sanitation, etc. But here, these souls do not have the talent nor have they developed themselves to plan the cities. They are not capable to make a master plan for a city, they just plan on a daily basis. Whoever comes with a request to make a building with their plan is approved by the authorities, provided applicant, pays enough bribe to the person who is approving.

'For example, here, anyone can become a builder or a developer who has a small sum of money and has contacts with the authorities. Then he joins with an architect who is a master in manipulation of the rules, and then approaches the authorities who are waiting for these type of clients, so that they can get huge bribes and they will sanction in whichever way you need the plan to be passed. The architect and the builder who have the plan for a building can get it passed with any number of flats that he wants in the building irrespective of the size of the plot, even though there is no playground for the kids and no space for parking. The buildings are also usually constructed in a small plot of land. Hence, it will be illegal to build more than a specified number of flats. To get that done, all that the builder needs to do is pay off the authorities. Once the building is ready to be occupied, buyer who has paid crores of rupees for each flat will have hardly one parking lot in the compound. But they will have three to four cars for each family.

'These are the same people who did not have even a car a few years back. But now, he believes that the more number of cars he owns, the higher his social status is. They are in a constant competition to show off their wealth and money. One for him, one for his wife, and one each for his kids to drop them to school (those unfortunate kids are not allowed to walk, the driver is forced by the parents to drop the kids in front of the school gate, whereby the kids become fat and unhealthy). Therefore, the rest of the cars are parked on the road as if it is their right.

'So what happens now? They are all forced to park the cars on the road; hence, they involuntarily yet forcibly use the road in front of their building. All the buildings on the road completely occupy the road that leads to a narrow foot path, which is constantly on repair. The authorities repair it once in every six months, so that they can gobble up more than half of the quoted price from the contractor. That is yet another drama!'

But I can see that some vehicles which are running here are made in this country.

'Yes, there are certain crooked and wise and smart souls among this chunk too. Do you know what they do? They travel to the western world, and find the newest items that are created by people in those developed nations. They manage to get permissions to copy that, and they agree to pay a share of the profits too. They come back and manufacture these here with the help of those bright engineers and sell them to those undeserved souls.

'Not a single thing made here is developed by these souls, not even a motor bike or a healthy loaf of bread! Not only that, the government that they formed after getting freedom from their earlier rulers and the politicians (by keeping the interest of the dirty industrialists) have closed this country from the outer world. They literally chained the entire population to their rules. Also, they forced people of this country to buy products of those industrialists who got the patent rights for old technology, which they bought from the western world and they keep dumping this on the entire country.'

CHAPTER 4

An Incredible 'No Man's Land'

It is a pity that these souls cannot even copy an idea properly, an idea which is thousands of years old.

Romans invented block locking stones, and they were used on the roads hundreds of years ago. It was only recently that the people of 'no man's land' got the idea to copy the same system. They started it off by manufacturing and installing it on some of the roads here and most of the foot paths too (the blocks are made in substandard materials due to which it starts crumbling in a few months, whereas western people make the same kind of blocks which withstand and remain in good condition for many decades). But it was all in vain. In a few days, the blocks started loosening and the stones started standing in vertical and horizontal positions! It is because they did not give a proper level ground before fixing the blocks. Who will be able to walk on those kinds of roads? Pity the old and weak that live in this land.

These souls have not been able to follow the simple system of road construction. Yes, it does not take much hard work. Romans have been doing this since thousands of years ago. By channelizing water flow through right mediums, water can be harvested instead of remaining stagnant on roads because all that it does is destroy the roads.

They have not made proper channels for the water to drain out. After every rainy season, the roads are completely destroyed by pot holes. They give out another contract to their panel companies in order to refill potholes and repair them. This becomes a cycle. This poor nation repeats the same process every year, and roads are mended year after year. The self-proclaimed journalists and other prominent people shout and cry against these situations created every year and the difficulties for the people, also the wasting of money etc. But none can think and suggest methods to solve the problem of water stagnation and also the use of substandard materials which are used by the contractors etc.

The highest rates of negative brains are found here. I say this because they invented the system of granting the public works by calling the tender of public projects and giving it to the lowest bidder. They have no idea that the lowest bidder will be all set to use the cheapest materials, low grade staff and workers. After sanctioning the work, the lowest bidder starts the work at a slow pace. He makes sure that he creates a rapport with the work supervisors, and ends up giving them money for benefits.

In this course, both the bidder and supervisor gain. Loss has to be incurred by the poor nation. Hence, a project that was supposed to be completed in twelve months with 100 crores of rupees will end up taking four to five years for completion, and the cost will be four to five times what was expected by the government. Moreover, inconvenience to the masses is not even taken into consideration.

CHAPTER 5

A Walk on the Footpath

There are hundreds of vendors crowded on these footpaths.

They cannot even construct a good footpath. Street vendors occupy foot paths by paying daily haftas (money) to the officials, so that they are not asked to leave. Moreover, footpaths are made in such a way that not even a fit and healthy man can walk properly on them. Authorities make footpaths with minimal consideration and sensitivity toward the common man. They make it in such a way that pedestrians have to climb up and down after every few meters. It is near to impossible for a blind man to walk on the footpaths in this land. Do I have to mention the plight of old and the weak?

Can't they construct a footpath without those steep steps? Why can't they make a small hump, so that the footpath continues without any hurdles?

The engineers and technicians in government departments are very poor thinkers and generally lack common sense. They might have secured seats in schools and colleges through caste reservations, and even got their jobs on this basis. All these factors rule people here. What intelligence do you expect from such people?

An interesting fact is that all the intelligent students fly abroad to study and work. They do not want to be here. They know that they will have a dignified profession and better life in other countries. Second grade students get jobs in foreign companies in 'no man's land'. They will be getting a decent income too. Third grade students are the street smart souls! They start a business or an enterprise. Fourth grade students get to work in the organization of the third grade and what is left over gets pulled in by the government!

Government officials are people with lesser caliber. The best example starts with the first Leader. He invented an idea to churn out the best brains from here and dispose them off this country.

He started an institution called IIT. A nationwide test will be held to find the best possible brains from various schools and universities across the country. Once they find the best kids, they get an admission into an IIT and provide the best possible education, which will be almost free of cost. The money for their education will be spent by the government. All the top grades are picked up with incredibly brilliant salaries, posh bungalows, and high status in western companies. Hence, all the clever ones leave the country. Yes, they got free education by government, and now they are all set to make a remarkable change in our western counterpart nations! This ceremoniously happens every year. They spend millions to get the best kids by the entrance exams, and then educate them by spending millions; and at the end of the year, 90% go to western countries and work for them. Forget about the mistake of that idiotic idea, but till now, not a single soul in this land could realize the error that they are doing and none can suggest a simple rule to prevent it by making the kids to sign up an undertaking that they will work in this land instead of running away from here and not contributing to this land.

CHAPTER 6

A Country that Breathes Corruption

Why is there so much corruption here? I saw it in other parts of Earth too, but this is insane!

Corruption is a way of life here. It is an accepted norm, and one can feel it in the blood of every soul who lives here. There is no harm in being corrupt here. Seeds of corruption are imbibed in the system of everyone through their own parents.

Here is an example. On the exam day, after making the child mug up his textbooks, parents take them to a corner of the house where their family God (an idol) is kept. They fold their hands and put a few coins and fruits to the idol, asking for success in the exam. So, what does the kid learn? By paying someone, known or unknown, he/she can get the work done. This remains stamped in their minds forever. This is exactly the same technique that they use later on in life too. And once the child grows up fully, he/she starts treating the government employee as his/her living God who can grant him/her what they wish instead of going through the process and rules prevalent in other parts of the world.

Having said all this, we must never underestimate the caliber of this land. The best possible negative brain can be found here. They are the ones who make rules for everything. In fact, they create so many rules almost every second week in all departments. The more the rules, the more confused the people get, by which they can make more money by bribes. Corruption becomes a natural consequence of it. For example, if you want to do the interior decoration for an office premises in this city (we shall start following up with a person who is trying to do his office done up, since we are not visible to their eyes, it is easy for us to follow him everywhere), the second day of the work is interrupted by a local authority who would come and visit the premises. He will ask the workers to stop the work.

Wondering how he came to know it so fast? Officers are paid to work in offices, but here, they move around. The securities in buildings are their main helpers. The officer will ask to inform about a new work that is happening. He offers a portion of the money as well. So now, it is your turn to go and meet the officer. The officer will say that since your office is certain sq. ft. area, you will have to pay a certain amount as bribe. Otherwise, he will not allow you to go ahead with the work. You can argue with him, but all that they will tell you is either you pay or stop the work and go to the court to get permission for a renovation. The bewildered owner will run to a lawyer, again, to be heartbroken. The lawyers will advise him not go to court because the procedure will take many years. Even his suggestion would be to pay some money to the officer and move on with life.

Here is another example. In all the developed countries, if you want to register any of your deeds, sale or lease with a registrar, the process is quite simple. You must pay the required stamp duty through Internet, scan, and post your papers. Then an officer will check whether the citizen has paid the required amount as tax or stamp duty to the government or not.

But here, both parties have to go to the office registrar. The officers would have kept a few agents who would loaf around in the same office. All you need to do is give the deed or agreement papers to the agents. They will take care of the rest. You must pay the agent. Since he has a tie-up with the officer, they will decide on the payment that needs to be done by you.

Usually, the fee is fixed according to your agreement value. Now, if you decide not to pay this bribe money and want to go to the law directly, then the officer will read your agreement, and will come out with at least a dozen mistakes and ask for many other supporting documents towards that property.

Okay. So you decide to go back, collect all the required papers, and come back after a few days. He will still point out umpteen mistakes in your papers. You will have to go back again and get it done. In the end, you just get fed up and decide to go to the agent.

CHAPTER 7

Divided by Religion, United by Hatred

Tell me. How did this land become unique from others industrially, culturally, and technologically? Why are these people here so insensitive to atrocities?

When 'no man's land' got freedom, the post-independence ruler and his subordinates wanted to make the country a socialist state because they believed that it would be nice if every human being is considered equal. And they decided that the people only need food and a mere shelter and a few clothing. ; they did not believe in progress and improvement, as they wanted to live in fool's paradise by saying that all are equal etc. (which is the policy of a socialist state). The cars were considered a luxury and of low priority too. It is also because the entire people here could believe and think only from a bullock cart era., but the West and a few other clever nations became industrial powerhouses, and they kept innovating new things for their people. Even though these rulers and government officials were traveling around the developed world and seeing new and better things, they decided that the people of this land did not deserve any better things. They refused them to the people of this land, but, of course, they used them for themselves.

Politicians and bureaucrats here do not know how to rule efficiently. They do not know what to do with the freedom that they received. These people wisely initiated the License Raj. According to it, if one wants to start a business, he/she has to go to the government office to get a license. The acquired license will mention about your production details, that is, how much you can own, and how much can be manufactured even if the demand is much more. At times, the license will be given only for half of the total demand, so that the authorities can control. Whereas in other countries, the authorities will give permission to the entrepreneur to manufacture any number of quantity, so that the cost of production will be much less, and they can sell at a better price not only in their land but also all over the world.

Remember what I told you earlier? Even though these folks do not have a developed brain for creative work, they have the brains to make devastating rules that can create obstacles for people who want to do a decent business.

This type of control will result in a situation where the entrepreneur has to approach them always, so that they can expect to be paid bribes. They need bribe for everything; they are seldom bothered about their actual salary.

    ✦   By now, you might think that the politicians and the bureaucrats are destroying this land. In fact, the truth is something else. The industrialist are the one who is controlling those politicians and bureaucrats. It all started after independence. This nation got freedom from the British. Later it came under the rule of a leader who got into the chair by mere luck and accident (not by the choice of people or by his own talent). In fact, he was born in a rich family and had never seen or felt the hunger and difficulties of the 80 per cent population of this land. After getting into the post of the ruler, he was living in a world of illusion. He refused to accept the reality of his land, which is reeling under poverty, and this nation needed the help of rich and developed countries. He created the dream system called *socialism*. He was the most right person to appoint the worst possible persons for the right job. For example, he appointed the most unsuitable people in charge of industry, defense, finance, etc. The worst appointment was for the work of making the constitution of the country. He looked at only the popular demands and not for the best result,

He appointed a person to make the constitution, just to appease the majority of the people of this land. The constitution thus written creates havoc even today.

The fact is that, no one is responsible as per the constitution (there are only dreams and promises of dreams) the common man is promised that he will get justice, but he or she has to spend many years, sometimes, a few decades, and also have to bear the expenses of a lawyer. It means 70 per cent of the common man is refused justice. The government officer has got all the rights and powers to do any wrong to the general public, but he cannot make a rule or take a decision to help them or make an improvement in the infrastructure or take a decision according to the changing times. On the other hand, he holds the discretionary power to put anyone in trouble if the common man does not heed to his demands (this encouraged and strengthened corruption). He used the discretionary power and threatened the common man. And if he/she doesn't heed to his demand, then the common man has to go to the said lethargic court to prove that he is right, which will take many years and drain out all his resources. So no one dares to offend the officer, instead, he pays it off.

The second worst appointment was in the defense ministry, every country sets up the defense to protect and also to store weapons as a deterrent to other countries that have evil motives. During World War II, their ruler had put up many factories to produce all kinds of weapons including aircrafts, tanks, guns, etc. When their ruler left they have left behind the factories and a well-trained army. But when the leader appointed this defense minister, who believed in peace and thought all the neighbors were peace lovers. He created his own fool's paradise and started roaming around the world and did not spend any time in his job as a defense minister. He ordered dismantling of all the factories and to reduce the number of military personnel to 1/3 rd of their strength. This nation has an immediate neighbor who believes in strength and respects others who are strong. They dislike weaklings. They noticed this nation is ruled by inefficient people who had given up their defense preparedness. So for the sake of an adventure for their military or as a training program on how to kill their enemies, they launched an attack and slaughtered many thousands of defenseless army men who did not even have proper guns or enough bullets to put up a strong defense. The most heart breaking and sad moment for the history was when the neighboring army poured in thousands into this land, the leader who was requested to send the air force to protect their soldiers who were getting slaughtered every minute, he refused to do anything about it, in his foolish hope of an end to the war and naïve thought of continuing relationship with his neighbor. He sat there without doing anything. The end result-after all those debacle and man made tragedies, this poor nation had to import billion worth of equipment every year (till now, they are not even capable of making a revolver or a bullet themselves). But again the developed countries are still selling their weapons which are obsolete and outdated, but this nation had to be content with these.

Needless to say, much about the industries minister. He and the leader believed in Socialism, but not in progress or technological research. They thus cut off the country from the outer world and paved the way for a few of their close industrialist buddies to take control of the whole business.

A few opportunist industrialists noticed this situation and took advantage of it. They went to the western world and approached some companies to give them the technology and permission to manufacture products like, cars, trucks, tractor, etc. Those wise companies gave them the oldest and outdated technology to these people and made them sign the document to give constant royalty money for it. Then these industrialists persuaded the first ruler to pass the law in the parliament that no other foreign companies can come into this land and sell their newer and better products. With the help of that law, they could keep making those outdated products and sell them to these people for many, many decades and make billions out of it. These are a few examples:1. Someone got the permission from a company called FIAT, which he named it here as PADMINI (the company gave a model which was outdated at that time). Another man went to get a car and named it 'Ambassador'. Through the mechanism of licensing, government could wisely give import orders, while giving license to in-house manufactures to manufacture only a small quantity. Soon the demand kept growing and supply was not matching. The system was like this, if you wanted an on-time delivery, you had to pay bribe. Otherwise, you could wait in the line indefinitely.

Politicians and concerned officials started minting cash from car manufacturers, while the shrewd industrialist kept making the same dumb cars for decades. The poor person here had no chance to get a modern car. Even when the world was going so far ahead with many types of newer and faster cars, these poor souls had to live with the same old ones.

To establish the foolishness of their clients, the smart industrialist would announce that newer cars would come to the market every year. And finally, they came with a change of bulbs in the headlight, or maybe with the bumper slightly twisted. The industrialist is not having buyers here; he makes victims here.

Look at the way in which the truck runs on the roads. The poor driver is sitting in a cramped place worse than a jail, and the steering is so hard that he has to use all his limbs to make even a slight little turn. The engine is under power, and if it has to climb a hill, it goes at a donkey's pace. They mainly carry goods in these trucks. That is manufactured by another crooked business group who could manage to get the technology from a developed nation which was around 1940 model and they kept making it and selling it for many decades.

Where are the politicians? Where are the lawmakers? Doesn't this country have all these?

It is the politicians and bureaucrats who created the system with the help from the industrialist, and planned roads filled with potholes and crates. The vehicles running on these roads are even worse. This is just what the ex-British prime minister said when 'no man's land' got freedom.

Power will go to the hands of rascals, rogues, freebooters, and all 'no man's land' leaders will be of low caliber and men of straw.

They will have sweet tongues and silly hearts. They will fight for power and 'no man's land' will be lost in political squabbles. A day would come when even air and water would be taxed in 'no man's land'.

They kept on increasing the number of licenses that were required to start a business here. For example, if a small entrepreneur wants to start a restaurant, with permission for liquor, he will have to get around twelve to thirteen different licenses for which he has to go through the agents appointed by those rogue government employees and pay the bribes.

Let me tell you something interesting. Here, there is no need for any basic intelligence or quality to become a politician. The only qualification needed is that he should be capable of creating chaos in the society, and offer and sell all kinds of dreams to the ignorant. The common people are mere cowards and dreamers. They just blindly accept everything and do not dare to question!

HEIGHTS OF COWARDICE

The entire land is filled with cowardice. Take a look at the individual who is walking on the street or standing and waiting for something. He will be so gentle, naïve, polite, and whatnot! But if the same person is with his friends, he will be a totally different person. He will be staring at all the people who are walking around him, and will speak out loudly to his friends to intimidate others and keep spitting around.

Try this. We must take the form of a human and go to one individual here and call him some abusive words. You must see what he will do and how he will react. We did this in the western world, and also in Africa. Out there, a few individuals slapped me when I called him a bastard. But most of them looked at my face and turned back as they thought that I am a mad man. No one came to me later. But look how people behaved here.

In no man's land, no one hit me or spoke back. What they did was they came back with people to beat us. When he (the guy who was abused) was alone, he did not have the guts to answer back. But he is capable of carrying the dirt/ anger in his mind for many hours and then distributes the same dirt and anger to his friends. He convinces them to come along with him and beat me up.

The politicians here are a reflection of the masses. So let me tell you about a politician who became the most beloved in this land. He maintains a few boys loafing around with him, at all the time. If there is a businessman or an opponent who does not listen to his request or is not ready to pay the monthly hafta, he sends his boys very proudly to break the other man's legs, and destroy his personal property! Then, he becomes a national leader and makes billions by doing the same thing over and over again. And yes! He makes more and more money to recruit more and more people into his circle. By doing this, he created the entire local population idle and lazy. Ironically, the wives of those local men are forced to work as maids and sweepers in others houses.

Why is that crowd over there, throwing black ink on that person's face?

Yes, those are the same bunch of thugs who just cannot accept the views of others, and they try to impose their ideology. They have no brain to understand other's opinion and have not learned to respect others.

But in other parts of the world, if a person does not agree with the other person, they sit and negotiate. Why can't they do the same here?

No man's land lacks sense and visualization. They are just a few steps above animals. They are primitive. Have you heard of an animal called skunk? When you go to catch him, he sprays his urine onto your face, which stinks so bad! These people do the same kind of action by putting ink or color on to those who opposes them. This is their way of protest.

CHAPTER 8

Good vs. Evil, Poor vs. Rich

I have heard about some rich men in this land, and their fairy tale stories of being rich in a short span of time.

Yes, what you heard is right. They are the most cunning men in the lot. They get ideas and technologies from western world. Then they approach politicians in their homeland and get the rules twisted, so that all the people in the country have to buy their products, and are left with no other choice! The masses literally become slaves to these companies.

Take a look at one of the biggest business houses. More than fifty years ago, the family members from this group went to the developed world, and got details of the model of a truck to manufacture it back home. This dates back to nearly six decades. This great family went on to make the same model trucks without any change for years. So even now, they manufacture the same trucks after decades! It is so primitive compared to automobiles in the other parts of the world. But people use it with no complaints. This business house believes that people in their homeland deserve only that much and they keep minting money out of an age old technology (which is not even theirs). Well, there is nothing surprising about it. This is no man's land!

They make the cartels and control the law makers and twist the rules. They get the copies of the new laws and plans in advance even before presenting them in their parliament. They manipulate the laws and lawmakers by paying bribes that even prohibit any other citizen in the country from inventing any other model of truck. Also they were not allowed to get technology from other countries and use it here.

CHAPTER 9

Entry of the Rulers

People here can always choose to have a good ruler who will adhere to the rule in the same way it works in other countries.

This land has been ruled by invaders and outsiders for centuries. And you know something? The country has always been better off when ruled by these outsiders under their leadership. For instance, centuries ago, the Afghanistan army came here and defeated an army that was five times bigger than them. They ruled here for many years. One good thing that foreign rulers did was creating a monument called Taj Mahal, which is one of the Seven Wonders of the World. Even today countless tourists from abroad visit this monument and remain wonderstruck. Even today, this poor nation can enjoy the benefits out of this great structure.

Later, some other invaders came. This time, it was from a place called England It was a few thousands who came, but could manage and defeat millions here as these inhabitants were fighting amongst each other like animals. (Also, the tactics and ideas were so primitive). Rulers here were busy with their extravagant life, luxury, and sex. The British too ruled this country for nearly 250 years. They were clever and business-minded, could make some remarkable changes in this land, and altered the land, which was fragmented into many pieces before their entry. It was literally the British who united this land, which is now called the 'no man's land.'

The British did a lot of investment in this land by making highways and railways across the country. The networking was so good that it had connectivity across the entire land. After the British left, sixty-seven years have passed and they could only increase the population, which has grown four times'

Another thing is that the English language, which was brought by the British still benefits this land. Western companies get their work done through young men and women in this country (there are a few companies called Infosys, Wipro, etc.) which make a kind of labour camp to recruit boys and girls who have studied and learned English. These companies make them do the work required by the western companies (Western countries cannot legally have slaves, so they use this method.).

Imagine, if the British had not made such remarkable developments during their period, this land would have been in complete darkness.

Take a look at the cities, roads, and buildings planned and implemented by the British nearly 200 years ago! They are still so strong. And whatever has been developed post-independence from the British era are already in a dilapidated condition.

The Taj Mahal was created by the Moguls. The iconic sculpture was the dream of Persians! Shah Jahan dreamt about it, asked his architect to put it in paper and then built it in memory of his wife.

In spite of a group of people who had opportunities to go abroad and become western educated, they had not been able to even copy an idea with perfection. Even an architect who returns to this land after western education is in a hurry to get into the corruption game and put all his energy in manipulating and cheating his own motherland.

So uncle, do you think that if the British had never left this land, perhaps the situation would have been better here?

This land was not ruled by the British government; it was ruled and controlled by a British company. They came to this land to trade and make money. They had their eyes on cotton and spices. Very soon, they understood that it was easy to rule people here and take control over them. They knew it would benefit their business plans too. There were more than thirty different states that were ruled by different kings. They were all fragmented and constantly fighting with each other. The kings were too lousy. All that they were interested in were sleeping, gambling, and indulging in luxuries and sex. Common man suffered in the hands of these kings.

The British were smart in foreseeing things. They invested on railways and roads. They built railways and highways, but by the nineteenth century, an alternative for cotton entered the market. Hence, from here, business and profits were flowing in to the British land at a much slower rate. There were no profits from it. Also, the British company had to spend a lot of money on roads and railways etc., but the company who was controlling the country was not making any more profit, as there was nothing much productive in this land. Therefore, they were contemplating to leave this land. In the aftermath of the Second World War, British were almost made bankrupt by the United States of America. USA had materials, instruments, weapons, and food. Now the British had no other choice than to give up all the countries that they had been ruling. But even now, these land dwellers were forced to believe that they got freedom because few people threatened the British that they will fast unto death and they used that sacred weapon. The truth was that more than half the countrymen men were living in starvation

The no man's land dwellers proved those wise words of the British prime minister and his foresightedness true- those words, which he said at the time of handing over the power back to those rulers.

Height of Lethargy

Here is something interesting. The British Empire was called an empire where ` 'the sun never sets', ` because they had colonies in every part of the world. British officials were appointed in all these colonies, and once these employees grew old, they would move back to their homeland. They had nothing else to do and had a lot of free time. They used to gather in open parks to spend time with their friends and families, to get sunlight as Britain lacks bright sunshine. They also wanted to engage in some fun. That is when they created a new game where one man throws a ball and the one standing opposite to him hits it back, so that the others who stand around the park can catch it. This game was an absolute pastime. It also helped them to be under the sun for some time. They introduced it to their other colonies too.

This game was perfect for these lazy souls, since there is nothing much to do the whole day and is a leisure activity. The game was lovingly called cricket. Today, everyone is crazy about cricket, and it is more like a religion to them. When there is a cricket match, people chuck work and sit in front of their TV screens just to see eleven men hitting, chasing, and catching a ball. This game is so silly, as one man throws a small ball to his opponent, the opponent who has a wooden plank to protect himself will swing the plank to protect him and also to hit the ball away. Then there are another ten men standing under the scorching sun and waiting for a chance to catch the ball, which was hit by the plank.

Strategically, the one who holds the plank gets the incoming ball once in every two minutes, and when he gets to hit the ball away from him, it is one out of four. So the ten men waiting to get hold of the ball each will get a chance to hold the ball in his hand once in every 15 minutes or so. But he is forced to stand and wait under the scorching sun to get his chance to touch the balls, the other millions patiently sitting in front of their TV screens watching this. Thus the height of lethargy and idleness was created.

Since this land is not capable to create a world-class sportsman or a world-class hero, the one who hits or catches number of balls are heroes to them. And yes, they are contented with it.

CHAPTER 10

The buildings, the architecture, they are all messed up.

Take a look at the prominent and successful architects in their cities. There is a story of an architect. He manipulated the rule for a land, which was reserved for the low middle group of people of no man's land. There was a strict rule to make houses less than 400 sq.ft for the lower middle class. You must know what he did by joining hands with the builder and with corrupt politicians and the so-called public servants? `Listen to this.`

The trio built houses that were around 400 sq.ft. (They made five to eight flats of the same size in every floor). They joined a few flats together and made it 1000–2000 sq. ft. and sold them to richer clients. And to beat the law, the flats needed to be lesser than 400 sq.ft. The rich buyer will have to sign a few agreements to this effect. This is how they cheat the country and their own people.

They are multimillionaires, and they are the prominent and most respectable developers and architects in the country. If you look at their architectural works, you will understand that they have not created anything new. All they have done is to copy some Italian designs. But in the end, it looks horrible too (the land which was reserved for poor section of the society has gone to the richer class, who twisted all the rules and made billions).

The so-called educated professionals also get into the game of corruption and encourage it. They get their work done with ease, don't they?

The more you cheat the country and its people, the more prominent and respectable you would be. That is how it works in this land. Media here are parasites who are completely in favor of the rich and powerful. In fact, most of the media which is supposed to be neutral and honest is owned by those politicians and the so-called industrialists, who use it for their benefit only. And the journalists are not free to do the work without bias, as they are employed and controlled by those mighty people. They too look only for their promotion and survival. They forget the real journalism, where you are supposed to be the mirror of the society.

A few years back, the government gave the contract of exploring potential underground oil and gas in this land to a western company (none of the local companies has the technology to find that out). The government had to pay the western company for their services. The western company could find a gas basin in the Bay of Bengal, and the details were handed over to the government. So how do you take this out and distribute it wisely amongst the people of this land? As a solution to this, they called for a tender to take out the gas and distribute it evenly. Again, none of the local companies could come forward because they did not have the kind of technology for it.

That is when a tricky businessman manipulated the laws and rules by corrupting the politicians and bureaucrats by paying them. They even got the most confidential policy papers from the parliament house by paying off the clerks. In fact, most of the law makers, called ministers and the bureaucrats already sold them to this huge family business. They believed that to be the noble way of doing business in this land.

They came forward and got the sole contract by corrupting the authorities by paying a few hundred crores! Hence, they got the sole right to take out the gas from an extremely rich basin. Then, they went to the western world, tied up with them for doing necessary drilling works for fixed fees. (They do not have any technology nor any idea of taking the gas out and distributing it The only talent they had was to manipulate the politicians and keep them under their payrolls.).

That was how they managed to get the right to drill the gas, which actually belongs to the inhabitants of this land. Now everyone has to pay for gas, which is actually their own! These industrialists cannot even create anything in life, but they make money by fooling their own people.

As I said before, in no man's land corruption is the accepted norm and the industrialist used it well by becoming the father and great grand fathers of corruption. They keep getting hundreds of crores from that gas deal, which they smartly acquired in the most cunning and inhumane way. The only talent they have is the knack to bribe politicians and buy government workers. They neither have any technology nor they could develop anything new in this world, but they can still be one of the richest men in the world, and they want to become richer by snatching wealth from their own brothers and sisters!

These industrialists make houses of many thousand sq.mts worth many billions of dollars. In the midst of all this, millions of families are forced to live in mere 100 or 200 sq.ft of shanties with no running water or toilets. Even the pregnant women have to stand in a queue for their turn to go to the toilets.

In other countries, the richest people created something or invented something new and provided it to the society.

By this way, they become richer; but here, you can find the rich people doing nothing new nor creating anything new except manipulating the rules, exploiting and grabbing the wealth of this nation for their own selfish ends.

There is another industrialist who bought an outdated three-wheeler technology from a western counterpart along with some other industrialists. They still manufacture the same shabby vehicles. The technology is so primitive; it pollutes the atmosphere, and makes loud noises creating noise pollution as well. Those who drive these vehicles are very ignorant, though arrogant, and uncivilized. They practice no discipline or driving etiquette.

Now this industrialist is still against policies for no man's land that opens up this country to the world. He believes that these souls are not entitled to better things in the world, and they want only their out dated products to be sold in this market. Also these three-wheeler is unfair on the road and creates problems to other vehicles as well. When everyone has to go straight, this vehicle can move in any direction as it has got only one front wheel. Therefore, more chaos on the roads!

Modus operandi of such people is quite unique. They keep paying constant bribes as money or as some other favors to the government officials. Then they manipulate these officials for their own professional benefits. It's easy and keeps happening. You can bribe a government official to get the crucial policy documents from government offices. Beat that?! (No need to rob it)

After making billions of money through crooked methods, what these people return to the society is very interesting.

The industrialist, once again manipulated to create a new rule allowing the companies to use certain portion of their profit toward hospitals or health-related activities for the benefit of the common people. In fact, that money which the government reduced is the tax, which is actually payable to the nation. The new rule has helped them to get more money from these hospitals, instead of giving subsidized treatment to the patients. From these activities also they makes millions—not a single poor or middle-class man can ever benefit from it. They still have to go to the dirtiest government hospitals and avail cheap treatment.

CHAPTER 11

People here look unhealthy and lazy

Yes, their food is spiced with masala, which is tasty to the palate, but bad for the stomach and the digestive system. After eating such heavy foods, the body requires more than 50 per cent energy to digest it. Hence, he/she, who eats this, becomes a couch potato

Women are being raped mercilessly every day here. Why does it happen here like this?

It happens every day, and it happens because their society adds fuel to it. Hear this. In every other part of the world, when a boy or girl reaches puberty, they have the freedom to choose their partner. It is completely up to them and their choice. They also have the freedom to choose their sexual life.

The hormone in a boy is active when he is twelve to fourteen years of age. He becomes aggressive and fights for existence. He wants to pass over his genes to the next generation, which is not his idea but it is planted in him by nature. The human has spent the maximum time, as per history, not in houses, but in caves (humans used to live in caves millions of years ago). They used to live in deep and dark caves. The male had to go for hunting, and there were times when they would take days to return, or maybe never return because they would be killed by animals or by the enemy.

Sometimes, men from other clans would invade and kill the males and children to have more women. The life span of an average man used to be less than twenty-five years! Hence, he was always in the rush to pass on his genes to the next generation. He could do this because the nature had created him with a string of hormones inside him. He was trained to be an aggressive animal.

This aggressive behaviour in man, as it is the rule of the nature, he can only be controlled and tamed by a woman. But here, society does not allow a girl to be with the person she loves, or the boy cannot go near her till they enter a sacred wedlock. Unfortunately, there is an aggressive person inside the boy, genes that had been transferred through him by this nature, and those genes are dangerous! Even though he is aggressive, he has to remain calm and quiet in front of the society. When he gets a chance to be alone with a woman, he turns out to be a wild animal that cannot control itself. That animal behavior is ruled by its inbuilt instinct and the law of the nature.

This society is lost in the wilderness and they cannot even understand the reason for it. They don't want to even think about it or find solutions. They cannot think why this crime happens mostly here when compared to other countries.

People here are like frogs in the well. Their eyes are closed, and they think what they have around them is the best.

Politicians, women welfare organizations, and moral police give their opinions that men should be punished severely. Well, there would be many other suggestions too. But no one spends time to think about the man who committed the crime, and the reasons that led him to do so. Media makes money out of it. In this land, media are like vultures. They wait for a bad death, accidents, or rapes so that they can flash it on their screens to make a livelihood.

They also forget that the culprit was raised by a mother who failed in her duties, and that he has a wife who was an utter failure in taming the animal in him.

Rape victims can be of any age here. From two years to seventy years. Rapists are unconcerned with the age of a woman. The more heinous, the News channels have something to feast on. They create breaking news, and they have a panel of nincompoops who would discuss the rape incident for hours on news channels. This is amusement to the public, who sit and listen to this filth for hours.

People here are extremely insensitive. So is the media.

No one wants to discuss the root cause of rape and what needs to be done to root out this evil. Women welfare organizations and moral police want to come in TV channels and keep raving about the rape incident. Advertising companies too have a gala time during a rape incident.

This land has reached a pathetic situation where TV channels are hunting for rape cases across the country, so that they can increase their TRP ratings and commercials. All news channel claims to be *numerouno*. But unfortunately, news channels compete among themselves. They claim to bring out the news first and that they have a skilled team and a seasoned reporter. But the fact is far away from this. The reporter would be an immature intern who does not even know the basics of good reporting, and the techniques he would have employed could be outdated. In their rush for covering the breaking news, reporters seem like they cannot even breathe while talking. But actually, they are repeating the same thing over and over again. No one will ever know whom they are kidding!

For example, let us imagine that the reporter would be in the spot where the rape has taken place. He/she will constantly try to extend his/her description of the incident for a few more minutes so that the senior takes notice of this gimmick. He/ she gets all appreciation. He /She may even get a promotion for mocking the people cleverly. Some other news channels, who failed to get the rape news would rush to an accident spot, which presents yet interesting breaking news.

Why is the media not responsible and accountable?

Now the latest trend is that if a crime is happening and you take a video of it and give it to a news channel, you would be handsomely rewarded and applauded. Through this one video clipping, the TV channel also gains TRP ratings and commercials, which means more money! But no one who was at the crime scene will stop the culprit from doing the crime. They would rather remain as passive spectators, busy planning on how would they get an interesting video clip of the scene.

Are there no rules, laws, and judges in this country?

The laws here are primitive because most of them were copied from the British laws. The laws are outdated and go back to nearly 100 years. The victim will have to spend many years to get justice. They have to spend a fortune and all their energy on winning the case, running after the cops and the courts.

As mentioned earlier, the clever and sincere ones are sucked in by foreign countries. The left overs hang around and enjoy facilities provided by the nation. In turn, they become a liability to the country rather than being an asset.

Even though the rules are copied from the British and the same rules are perfectly working in Britain, you may wonder why it does not work here. It won't, because this land is full of undisciplined souls.

It is hilarious to see the lives of the justice providers and officials in no man's land. But in other countries and abroad, even a governor lives in his own house, or sometimes in a house allotted by the government. He will drive his own car and go to office, but in no man's land, the governor lives the life of a king. With more than 100 workers and security staff, government has to spend crores on maintaining one state governor. His job is nothing but attending inaugurations, state gatherings, and parties.

People choose the most irresponsible politicians.

In this country, the politicians live life king size. He will appoint loafers to get all the dirty work done. If someone stands against him, they will be beaten up by the loafers. Hence, no one will question the cunning politician. Also, they can use the officials to do their dirty work as they hold the right of transfer and promotion. Thereby, the officials become their obedient servants too.

These souls can be trampled over by anyone and ruled by anyone. A small British company that came all the way just to do some business took over the entire nation. They could control and rule. All you need to do is promise them something. The British offered money and arms to the kings. They promised that these arms and money would help the kings in fighting their neighbors within the country. The British used this little trick which could have worked on kids. But look here, it worked on the kings. But now, the ruling politicians are doing the same trick by offering the people free food and everything else.

In other nations, the politicians promise to the people more jobs and jobs for all. They tell the people that there is no free lunch, whereas in here, the politicians offer them free food, free house etc and encourage idleness and lethargy.

After the British left and handed over the power to the unscrupulous politicians, they still continued the same method of selling dreams to the citizens. They even offered free food; free TV, free computer, and the ignorant believe this. No one has the slightest idea whether to question or think how the politicians can give it free. The worst of all is the reservation for jobs and education. It means that they are hell bent to make the country more inefficient. The masses are blind and ignorant. They accept this.

They do not question the situation because they are ignorant and blind. After every election, the same thing continues. It is like a cycle. These souls do not believe in self-esteem or self-respect. They ask God to provide everything for them, and they are happy with what God supposedly gives them. Just like how they beg to God, they beg to these politicians too. In other parts of the world, the masses believe that they have to take care of themselves and that they have to give the government a share instead of begging the government to give them something.

Here, some even take a weird shaped stone and put some color to it. Tell the masses here that the stone has divine powers and that if you pray to the stone, you will get all that you need, they would believe it. There will be thousands and millions who would be standing in front of it, folding their hands, offering fruits, gold, and coins.

The old buildings look divine. They are so beautiful. They are there in every nook and corner of the country.

The architects from this land have not done anything for this country, Whatever you see here has been made by the Persians or British.

Here, the architects are only capable of finding loopholes in the law and rules of the city. They are experts in bribing the officials. They become middle men between wrongdoers and government officials. They prefer cheating the masses and laws. The most successful architect in this land is not the one who creates beautiful buildings, but the one who can find loopholes and twist laws and even convert the land, which has been allotted for the poorest or for a garden or playground.

These people destroy the cities with their greed. They make millions and spend their life in luxury and foreign trips. They become heroes of architecture and people look up to them.

In this land, no one can digest power in the right way. For instance, if you elect someone as secretary of a small housing complex or apartment, he starts behaving like the owner of the building from the very next day that he gets elected. He starts yelling at the security and brings new laws. He does not realize that he is just being plain ignorant.

All like to make new rules and new laws.

CHAPTER 12

Food, Health, and Care

Why people are least bothered about their health here? They do not seem to be interested in managing themselves well?

In no man's land, when it comes to the health care, the industrialist treats this noble cause as a pure business to grab from the sick and dying

With the help of politicians and beaurocrats, they manipulate the rules. If a company spends a certain amount from their profit towards the health care to buy a hospital that is already running full-fledged, or they make a new hospital in their own name or their mother's name, they can get tax benefits and tell the world that they are into the noble work. But behind the whole thing, they charge extraordinary high fees from each patient who visits. And continue this practice as an industry to make millions.

All the money belongs to the masses of no man's land. But with this weird law, smart people can use it on ventures to gain more money and make profit. Not a single ordinary citizen will benefit from it. The people of no man's land still have to go to the dirtiest of government hospitals that offer the most pathetic treatment ever. Not only is that, the doctors are those who gained entry into these hospitals by special favors and reservation, not by their talent. They are unable to provide the treatment, instead, they too get into the money making activities like sending the poor patients to the nearest laboratories for various tests, so that they can get kickbacks from those private laboratories. Yes, the same government hospitals too have got the equipment, but those either are not working or are outdated. After all they have been purchased through the government's system of purchase, which ensures the lowest quality.

No man's land has earned a few names from its counterparts. Some of them are the 'rape nation', 'dirtiest country', and most 'undisciplined country' etc. In the last sixty-seven years, ever since the British left, these are the only names that they could possibly earn! Even they made their so called sacred river into the dirtiest river in the world.

In all major cities, the population has risen twenty times more than when the British left no man's land. But still, in no man's land, they are using the same water pipes and water systems that were created and established by the British. There are many hundreds of departments that they could create, but no additional work or any improvement has been done.

So every year, citizens have to face water shortage. The department heads are only capable of increasing the tax burden on the citizens. No one has any idea of how to minimize the wastage of water, or how to use the existing infrastructure in a better way.

In all the major cities, they face water shortage because the supply system is more than eighty years old. It was made by the British for one-tenth of the population of today. People in no-man's-land are still continuing with the same infrastructure, and they are not capable of making anything new to increase the supply capability.

They are not even able to keep their water systems running without leakage and wastage of water. Often, the water pipelines burst due to bad maintenance and precious water is wasted. That is when water mafia arrives at the scene. They are like scavengers. They exploit the situation, and the money is shared between the government officials.

Government officials ignore complaints on water shortage, and make sure that they don't maintain the pipelines properly. Water mafia carries water in the dirtiest trucks, and government employees help them with this, but only from behind the curtains. Due to these old trucks, traffic gets stagnated on small roads and things get worse. In fact, most of the water suppliers get their trucks filled with water from the same city water supply system, carry it, and sell it to the buildings and hotels.

In cities, people wash cars with drinking water and waste millions of litres when there are lakhs who are dying of thirst. Look at that employee cleaning his boss's car with drinking water! This must be made a criminal offence. Unfortunately, in spite of having many water departments, none of the officials are able to see this.

I saw a lot of cosmetic advertisements on the way. Why are people here obsessed with beauty?

The West wanted to dump their beauty products in no man's land because it is harmful for the human body and skin. Since it is difficult to sell such products in their own countries, as the women there are more pragmatic and level-headed, the next best option was to bring them to no man's land.

Western companies control beauty pageants. When they wanted to enter no man's land, they picked up a girl. They did makeup on her and made her look attractive. Then, they declared that she was Miss World! Alas, that was enough for the 600 million odd women in this country to copy that. Everyone wants to be beautiful.

Next, West made sure that beauty parlors were started in nooks and corners of the country with their products. Now, women spend all their time and money at the parlor, applying chemicals on their face and body just with the dream to look younger and beautiful!

Similarly, if they want to sell their aerated drinks, they pay huge sums of money to the cricketers, and make them hold an aerated drink in their hand. This appears on TV channels. That is enough for the millions in no man's land to follow suit.

Let me tell you something about the medical world here.

They are the worst. The medical degree that they have earned does not have any value in other parts of the world, and that is purely because no one in the world trusts them or their education. Some clever souls go abroad, study properly, try to settle down there, serve the people who are from the no man's land, make money, and live a comfortable life. In there, they have to acquire more degrees to be recognized as a doctor in that country. The funniest part is how they select the doctors in this land. First, the government have imposed some rules that 50 to 60 percent of all the medical seat quota are reserved for the so called downtrodden people, identified by the cast where the child took birth. These reserved students have the advantage of qualifying in the entrance exam with a lesser performance. The balance 30 or 40 per cent is selected by the college management by some kind of tender, based on the paying capacity of the students. This method of selection ensured that the worst of students got admitted and the really bright and deserving were dumped. The left over ones, who are here, are available for a mere few hundred bucks. If you want a fake sick leave certificate, it is easy. Just go to a doctor and pay him a few bucks and he will give you a certificate with whatever disease you desired! Cheating and lies are rampant in the medical world too.

If you are a patient who wants to visit the doctor, he will ask you to take many a scan. For a person who has lived a few years, wear and tear of the body is natural. Hence, the tests that you have taken will reflect this. That is when the doctor comes into power. He makes you feel scared, and he will ask you to take more tests with specific names. Remember, for every single test that the poor soul is going through, the doctor is getting a cut from the lab.

Then, the doctor will prescribe a few medicines. He will ask you to get medicines from certain companies, and those companies will be giving him commission, sponsoring for his foreign trips, buying his family expensive gifts, and so on. Yes, this does happen in no man's land!

If you go to a doctor in other countries, they listen to you; and after a thorough check-up, they will ask you to take only the required tests. Once the problem is diagnosed, they will ask you to take medicines for the diagnosed disease. If you are fine, they ask you to go home and move on with life. And if a patient is found to be suffering from a particular disease, which cannot be treated and the death is certain in a few months, then the doctor will tell the patient to go back home take some pain killers and enjoy the rest of his life.

Do you want to know what the doctors here do? They keep treating you. You become the provider of their meat, bread, and butter. In the end, they will say that, they have tried all the possible treatment options on you (even after knowing that the patient has only a few months to live) but cure does not appear to be possible, and now you can be taken back home or put on ventilator in the hospital. But by then, your pockets would be half empty, if not fully empty.

For liver, they give you a medicine. For lungs, there is another test. Heart, another, and the tests go on. They know that the medicine they give for liver will affect the kidney. Then he can ask you to buy more medicines. This game goes on and on...

CHAPTER 13

The City

Officials must be stricter. Laws must be implemented. Maybe the situation would change.

There are hundreds of departments that they have created. All that they can do is create more laws and more departments.

There is no infrastructure here. If someone tries to make a bridge, which is necessary to connect two places, some will object and delay the process. There is a road here named Peddler Road. It is extremely congested, and millions of people suffer every morning and evening trying to cross the road. The nation loses so much fuel in this process. When the government told the masses about this problem, a woman said that she would rather migrate to Dubai if the bridge project has to go ahead. Following her objection, the government backed out from building the bridge. Now, millions are suffering and heavy traffic causes pollution and burns thousands of ltrs. of fuel too.

If people here want a world-class facility, and wish to improve, then they will have to bring engineers and architects from Britain or Germany and make a new master plan to get the cities redrawn. That is because none of the engineers in no man's land is capable of efficient work and they are not capable to envisage the future and qualities in life. They all live with ego and short sightedness etc.

Officers cannot take a decision. They do not even have the efficiency to make rules, such as vehicle parking rules. They don't have the courage and integrity to stop the people from misusing the foot path, but their greed and selfishness drive them to take a few hundred as bribe to let such things happen under their nose.

The public transport, which is usually a three-wheeler, makes all kinds of menace on the road. It carries only two to three people and creates all sorts of chaos on the roads. They are strictly undisciplined and difficult.

This needs to be banned. Instead, a vehicle, like a jeep, must be allowed for public transport. It can carry at least twelve people, and will reduce the traffic to one fourth within a day. But no one will take any such decision because these three-wheelers have working unions, and are supported by politicians who want votes from that ignorant bunch.

The ministers who are in charge of development are from the interior villages. They impose the same village rules on cities too. For example, a bunch of pretty girls who are denied education for some reasons, wanting to earn a living decides to have a job by dancing and making others happy. That is when the minister will say that it has to be banned because it is against the culture.

In other parts of the world, this is an entertainment and has got nothing to do with culture. Along with solving the problem of unemployment, it also makes men more used to women's company, and hence, be cool with it. What happens in no man's land is sad. Men here are forced to jerk off or look out for women to rape. No women's associations fight for these poor women who want to make a living from entertainment!

Men here have zero respect for women. Also, women here refuse to show their strength to men. Women do not want to tell men about their needs and what they want in life. They prefer hiding it. They make sure men do not ever understand what they want because that is how society or culture here works!

This is the only country that keeps raving that women are fragile and needs to be protected. But atrocities against women happen here most because no respect is given. Fake rules are passed very often. But from their hearts, there is zero respect for women. Women are also to be blamed. They are dumb because they keep asking for rights, but they cannot work for their rights or get them by being bold. No man's land is blessed with 90 per cent cowards, and the balance 10 per cent who are parents of cowards.

Instead of working for their daily bread, people from no man's land expect Gods to feed them. They have dozens of Gods in their houses. They expect their children to pass exams with the help of Gods who are sitting in their living rooms. They prefer to bribe Gods so that their kids pass the examination! Here comes the dirty-minded politician, who understands the situation, and he becomes a living God and offers them everything for free, and those ignorant accept that promise and follow him.

People here prefer living in fool's paradise, and they present their bad deeds as glittering new ones. For example, if you ask them why they cannot build proper footpaths or roads, they blame it on things that are unimaginable. People in no man's land cannot even make a proper footpath or proper roads. They blame it on corruption or whatever else they can think of. If you ask them more, they counter argue and blame it on air, rain, water, and whatever they can think of.

They boast that 20 per cent of the work force in NASA and few other esteemed companies are the people from no man's land. They do not realize that people from no man's land who are working in such places are mere workers, and those are the companies which lured the best possible brains from this land and used them as workers.

When foreign companies like Pepsi or Coca Cola wants to target and expand the market in this land, they assign a CEO from no man's land and asks him to go to their own countries and capture the markets. They are just mere pawns. But people in no man's land take it as a credit and boasts about it.

SYCOPHANCY

These people are not only cowards, they are sycophants too. Look at those people falling on the feet of a politician, who is sitting on the chair. He just got elected as a minister. The people falling on his feet are just expecting some favor from him, which may or may not happen. But they are willing to stoop down in front of anyone.

Also, look at the crowd gathered and waiting for hours. That is the place where shooting is going on. Since they don't believe in reality, a few clever souls understand this situation and make films for these souls, which are like day dreams. The prettiest and richest girl falling in love with an ordinary man and they both fight against all odds and kill all villains. Finally the happy ending and they both start living in paradise.

Here, talent is not required to become the hero or heroine. What is required is that he/she should be the son/daughter of an actor. That's enough for you to become the next hero/heroin. The ignorant are not watching their talents; they just want to be carried away into the dream world. Nothing else matters to them. And since the society is so strict against the women expressing their real feelings, their beauty and body, as it is the rule of the nature (in the animal kingdom and birds world, the female always try to attract and seduce the male with its body and beauty) and here it is banned, the deprived males are mostly frustrated. But in the movies, these actresses who are not talented are allowed to expose their body, which is more than enough for the men folks.

Each city has some tale. Where this place is called 'God's Own Country'? I am eager to know if God really likes that place.

In certain area, the inhabitants claim that they are in 'God's Own Country' and they boast and claim that they are 100 per cent literate, but in reality, they are the most lowest in the matter of common sense and other various things.

Hear, when we walk on the roads, we can see people sitting in tea stall verandahs, doing nothing but engaging in small talks, and reading the trash in newspapers. They discuss the same thing over and over again for many hours. When you walk by, they stare at your face. They even refuse to blink because they are so involved in staring at you.

Look at the buffalo grazing in the grass. When we are near him, he raises his head and stares at us, and then goes back to chewing the grass. Don't you see a similarity? At least the animals will go out, fetch food, and feed themselves. People here cannot even do that, they just wait for the government to give them everything free of cost.

All that, these people can do the whole day is sit idle and gossip. They expect the government to feed them and provide them food and shelter, and they are happy not doing anything. Smarter are the ones who offer these people all these, and get votes every year and get elected ad rule them.

People in 'Gods Own Country' have invented something called 'Nokkukooli'. It means that people get paid for watching others do the work! The funny part is that it has got legalized as well. So there are a few people who work, and then there are others who stare at them working and still get paid for that. This happens only here.

Their main hobby and work is staring at others and gossiping. Hence, you can assume that they are 100 per cent employed for staring work and they deserve pension and salary for the same.

People here are against business houses coming up. They just do not want people putting up business houses or starting manufacturing units. Few who wish to work and build a career will have to migrate to the Gulf countries and work for the Arabs.

They want to prove that they are the frogs living in the wells. They proudly call this place 'God's own country.' You may wonder which God is ever ready to take the ownership for such a stupid bunch of people.

They believe that everything is equal. They think that all men are equal when it comes to talents. Only the circumstances make everything different. With that sort of thinking, they have no respect for others. When a man is ignorant and idiotic, he thinks that everyone is equal. That is when he forgets to respect others.

CHAPTER 14

It is sad to see this. Why are these people not able to change or resolve the problem and manage it with a better system like in the western world? I have a few questions. No man's land is using the same set of rules and regulations that are used in countries like the UK. But why is UK doing well when compared to no man's land? UK is clean and justice is provided to everyone without doubt. The majority of their people are prosperous and they have a high standard of living. But no man's land is getting worse with the same systems.

The system is not bad. It does not really hinder the progress of the country. It is the people and their poor caliber that disrupt progress here. The attitude and thinking pattern of a society play a crucial role in the development of a nation. If a nation has to grow, then the people of that nation need to accept and respect the system, but here, no one wants discipline or have respect for the system.

In no man's land, people with self-esteem and pride are less. Most of them have an inflated ego. Many, by nature, are cunning. They do not have a pro-active approach like people of other nations. They only react to situations like animals. That does not, in any way, help to achieve progress.

People here are obsessed with breaking rules. That gives them some sort of pleasure. They feel that they are superior when they jump even a traffic signal and spit in public places. It makes them feel greater than anyone else.

Do I need to speak more about government employees and politicians? They concentrate all their energy on getting bribes. They are competing amongst themselves to see who will get the maximum amount of bribe in a day! And then, they sit around and spend their energy thinking of how to spend the ill-gotten money.

The system is totally messed up. There are many bloodsucking industrialists. Due to such insensitive people, along with corrupt politicians and bureaucrats, it is the people of the country who are going to suffer. Their suffering is going to increase manifold. Can you suggest any better ideas that the people in no man's land' can follow so that the underprivileged and downtrodden people here can hope for better days?

COMPETITION

Competition is the way of nature and it's in all creations. It is from this force every new idea or a product comes out.

The dwellers of no man's land too are in competition, but they choose its wrong side. They have a neighbor who think and live the life in the same way as in no man's land. After all, they both were ruled by the same outsiders for a very long time. Ever since the foreign rulers left this area, both the nations remained in constant war and conflict for silly reasons. Even though more than 70% of the populations in both the nations live in utter poverty without running water and a proper shelter, the governments of both the nations spend their wealth and savings in buying the outdated and scrapped weapons from the western countries. In fact, those countries were planning to discard and destroy those outdated weapons, as they were obsolete and many decades old. If these two nations had not bought them, the West would have been forced to spend billions to destroy them as they had become useless and expensive to maintain.

Also, these two nations are spending their entire savings in making atomic bombs and shout at each other that they have more number of bombs than the other. Also, they boast that they have the technology to make this nuclear bomb. They want to take credit for it. In fact, a twelfth standard science student can make this type of dirty bomb in any part of this world. There are claims

and counterclaims that one is better than the other in
doing the destructive things in life.

Again, they are very proud of boasting themselves that
they have the technology to make missiles, which can
carry those dirty bombs and destroy the neighbor. Every
second month, each claims that theirs is bigger and longer
than the others. Thus they keep making bigger and
longer missiles and compete in the same foolishness, but
the reality is that, both cannot make even a simple motor
bike or a car or a good quality loaf of bread for their
people. Not only are they capable of it, but they don't even
make an attempt. The funniest part is that the ignorant
people of these nations neither have enough food to feed
their family nor a proper house with minimum facilities
like proper toilet and running water, but they feel happy
and contented with the government's claim of such atom
bombs and missiles to destroy the neighbor.

All those developed nations use the atomic technology to
produce electric power and provide it to their people. Unfortunately these two nations do not have the technology
nor have any idea of how to make electricity from the
atomic energy. So they beg and request the developed
nations to help them, as more than 50% of their people
live without electricity.

PREY AND PREDATOR

The law of the nature once again gets proved here, as no one is the ultimate predator. The West sells all their innovative goods and technology to the no man's land and into all other such nations, to makes money for their luxurious life in their land and they make their land clean and comfortable. But the dwellers in this noman's land are ignorant and cannot use the items invented and made by the West. For example, they misuse plastic, the cars and chemicals, etc., and scatter them all over the nature. They have no methods for their safe disposal. This eventually leads to air and water pollution. The signs of global warming are already seen. This is going to hit the West who thinks that their part of the world is safe.

And also, the medicines, which the West invented and manufactured, have started creating havoc in this part of the world. For example, for many thousands of years, people used to produce a dozen in each family, but the nature had its own control mechanism. But now, these medicines, in these parts of the world, are preventing the nature to have its control on the population growth. In the last seventy years or so, the population has grown four times and this huge population keeps migrating into the western world as workers or employees and swelling up the population there. Once again, those undisciplined lot creates havoc there. A few of them become terrorists and they will try to eliminate the same western people who had given them the comfort and living rights in their world.

Thus this part of the world has also started getting into a chaotic situation. During our next trip, we shall see what happens.

Solutions

UNCLE, why these people cannot change or resolve the problems and manage them effectively? I have a few questions:

1. (a) Since they are incapable to rule the land themselves which can only lead to more and more chaos, why not any western country come back and rule them again?(b)This land too is using almost the same rules and regulations which are being used in UK. In fact these rules were copied from those foreign rulers. With the same rules and regulations, UK is doing well and they are clean and they provide justice and prosperity to their people. They have also developed themselves to a very high level. On the other hand, this land is going southward with the same system?

2. Due to the senseless application of the rules, a few bloodsucking industrialists, along with the help of politicians and bureaucrats, the poor people are suffering and the sufferings are only going to

increase. Can you suggest any better ideas so that the underprivileged and the downtrodden can have a hope for the future?

Answer to point (a) of your first Question:- No clever western country will come here to rule them again. In fact, they are already ruling them with their technology and products. Imagine, if we intend to rule a land, what do we expect to do (a) to sell our ideas and our products; (b) to have cheap workers, right?

Now the westerners are selling all their products like cars, mobile phones, cameras, even the bicycles. They are recruiting the best possible talents and brains for their factories, and they lure them by offering better houses and bigger salaries and take them to their land and make them work.

About your second point at (b), it's not the system that is bad. With the same system you can make the country progress. The problem is the people, their attitude and their thinking pattern. In this land, there is no one with self-esteem. They have no proactive approach compared to the western people. Instead, as I mentioned before, they are reactive like animals. They are law breakers, lack civic sense, pride for the nation and above all integrity. The country has a high corruption perception index. The people put all their energy to secure bigger and bigger chunks of money illegally.

Answer to your second Question:-

Even if I give a few suggestions, these people are not capable of understanding them. Nor are they capable of implementing them as the British Prime Minister Churchill predicted. Yet, since you asked me for your learning, I shall suggest a few things:

1. First and foremost, the practice of sending out the brainy people to western countries and companies should be stopped and they should start providing them with good facilities to live with dignity. (They have developed a system where all are considered equal, the brainy, the ignorant, the anti social elements to be stopped and make a system to pay as per the capabilities and out put of the people, also to promote accordingly)

2. Stop recruiting the candidates on the basis of religion and caste. Place the right and the deserving at the right place, not on the basis of reservations. The undeserving will not only be unable to produce results, but can cause serious damage by doing nothing and causing the able person to follow the suit.

3. Stop providing free money and free items to the idle and lazy (by this system, they are only increasing their number.) Even the birds and worms in this world go out and fetch their

food, but, here, the politicians offer freebies and the people expect everything free. This only encourages laziness. The ignorant and the lazy accept it. Do you remember when we were traveling to this Earth, we could see a great wall, thousands of miles long and this is the only one thing anyone can see from the outer space which is made by human beings. That is called The Great Wall of China. The disciplined people of that country made it. They may not be equal to the westerners, but they can come very close to them by this good quality of discipline and obedience. Unfortunately, these two things cannot be found here. They have to make a strong system to discipline them. For example, the so-called public servant, when they get recruited for a government job or when the politician takes oath, they have to be made to sign an undertaking that if they get caught with charges of corruption or negligence of duty, they should be sacked immediately and punished by making them to do free work for the nation.

4. All the posts from and above the level of commissioner in all departments should be given to western nationals, as they are not corrupt (99% is not corrupt because they have the self-esteem and self-confidence, which is lacking in this land) Their present officers, for example, even a commissioner, instead of spending his brain to

do something new and something better for the country, he spends all his brain, time, and energy for appeasing his superiors and politicians to safeguard his post, and also for future promotions.

5. Bring western architects to this land and give them each a city to make a master plan, and then let them give the work to international standard companies to develop roads and other infrastructure. Stop giving the infrastructure works to the existing contractors who are nothing but manipulators.

6. Make every officer and government worker and politician accountable. Now they have a system as I narrated earlier. For a simple permission to start a small restaurant or a factory they have made a system of sending the file to more than a dozen people and finally, no one is answerable. If a factory violates some laws, you cannot catch one person as responsible for giving the permission. But all have taken money, and all have given the permission. By changing to the new system of making one officer responsible, even if he takes money, he is responsible and answerable to the nation.

7. Remove the power from the politicians to be the head of the department (now an uneducated arrogant silly politician can even become the head

of any ministry including industry or education). Since they are elected by the people, put them into a committee only to act as watchdogs for the bureaucrats for implementation of rules and regulations, so that the bureaucrats and other government workers are free to take their decisions for the country.

8. Remove the luxury from the judges and implement strict rules to them to finalize and give verdict in all cases of litigation within certain days. Then the lawyers will not be able to manipulate the law and the system. For example, for any case, on a given day of hearing, the lawyer of one side comes and requests for an adjournment for a few months. The judge agrees to it and sometime even gives an extension of many months. And next time, the lawyer comes with a medical certificate (even though sometime its fake), and again requests the judge for an adjournment for a few months more. The lazy half sleeping judge is more happier to give the adjournment than doing his/her responsibilities. The justice seeker keeps spending money for many, many years. The cunning lawyers enjoy their luxury life by doing nothing, and litigation keeps piling up.

9. Even though the democratic system is the creation of the West, many countries have adopted the same system including this no man's land. But

they made a mess out of it. For example, the Prime Minister of the country, who is the supreme leader is not elected by the people but elected by the representatives who got elected by the people. After the election, the representatives who got elected sit together and start bargaining and negotiating, and then they find a person as their prime minister. Since those few hundred elected people choose him as prime minister, the prime minister is only answerable to them. So he starts appeasing them by satisfying their demands. In fact, he is being constantly being blackmailed by them, as his very existence depends on those few hundred men. He is not at all accountable to the whole nation, nor he have to bother about it. He will spend his energy and time to keep those few hundred men happy instead of thinking about the country.

Somehow they found the best possible method to find the most undeserving person for the right job and eliminate the deserving ones. This practice has to stop immediately, if the nation has to survive.

Now it's time for us to move on to another planet, which is a few million light years from here, which we can travel in a few seconds as per our time schedule.

Dear uncle,

I found this tour very interesting, and I wish to come again. Yes, we saw nothing but confusion and lack of direction in this land. But is there any hope???

Yes my dear, I missed to tell you a point that, there are a few leaders with integrity and positive approach who are talking loud and working hard. They are the hope. They will put this land and its inhabitants on a progressive path. So let us hope and see the outcome during our next visit.

Lightning Source UK Ltd.
Milton Keynes UK
UKOW06f0559191116

288015UK00001B/3/P